THIS BOOK BELONGS TO

....

Copyright © 2015

make believe ideas ltd

The Wilderness, Berkhamsted, Hertfordshire, HP4 2AZ, UK.

www.makebelieveideas.com

THE UGLY DUCKLING

Written by Helen Anderton

Illustrated by Stuart Lynch

make
believe
ideas

Reading together

This book is designed to be fun for children who are gaining confidence in their reading. They will enjoy and benefit from some time discussing the story with an adult. Here are some ways you can help your child take those first steps in reading:

❋ Encourage your child to look at the pictures and talk about what is happening in the story.

❋ Help your child to find familiar words and sound out the letters in harder words.

❋ Ask your child to read and repeat each short sentence.

Look at rhymes

Many of the sentences in this book are simple rhymes. Encourage your child to recognise rhyming words. Try asking the following questions:

❋ What does this word say?

❋ Can you find a word that rhymes with it?

❋ Look at the ending of two words that rhyme. Are they spelt the same? For example, "crash" and "splash", and "beak" and "sleek".

Reading activities

The **What happens next?** activity encourages your child to retell the story and point to the mixed-up pictures in the right order.

The **Rhyming words** activity takes six words from the story and asks your child to read and find other words that rhyme with them.

The **Key words** pages provide practice with common words used in the context of the book. Read the sentences with your child and encourage him or her to make up more sentences using the key words listed around the border.

A **Picture dictionary** page asks children to focus closely on nine words from the story. Encourage your child to look carefully at each word, cover it with his or her hand, write it on a separate piece of paper, and finally, check it!

Do not complete all the activities at once – doing one each time you read will ensure that your child continues to enjoy the story and the time you are spending together. Have fun!

Mummy Duck has ten round eggs,
all tucked up in her nest.
The eggs go CRACK! The ducklings hatch,
but one's not like the rest.

This duckling isn't yellow
but rather grey instead.
"He's not the same. He needs a name,"
says Mum, "I'll call him Ned."

"Ned is ugly. Ned's so big!"
tease the duckling brothers.

Thinks Ned, "It's true.
What can I do?
I'm not like the others."

In the pond the ducklings learn
to swim in one neat line.

But with a SPLASH, poor Ned goes CRASH
right through the ducklings nine!

Then it's time to learn to QUACK,
  but Ned shouts, "HOOT!" with glee!
The ducklings laugh, and feeling daft,
  Ned sulks behind a tree.

"Hoot!"

QUACK!

Ned decides: "It's time to go –
I'll find a different flock."
And off he roams, so far from home,
with just his favourite sock.

13

First he asks some dancing geese,
"Please, can I join your team?"

The geese say, "No, you'll spoil our show.
But why not try upstream?"

Next he asks some hopping frogs,
"Please, can I join your crew?"

"If you can hop or belly flop.
   If not, try somewhere new."

Then Ned asks a magpie pair.

But on a sign they write:

× × × × × × × × ×
No ducks allowed –
and three's a crowd.
× × × × × × × × ×

Thinks Ned, "How impolite!"

As the moon and stars shine down,
Ned feels so out of luck.

A tear he weeps before he sleeps.
Poor Ned, the ugly duck.

He stays inside the sock for weeks.
Then one day, by surprise,
a noise wakes Ned, and from his bed,
an awesome sight he spies.

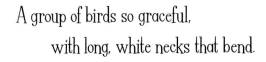

A group of birds so graceful,
    with long, white necks that bend.

They welcome Ned with wings outspread,
    and say, "Come, join us, Friend!"

21

Shyly, Ned swims to the birds
and asks, "How can this be?
For I'm so plain – please, do explain:
just why would you pick me?"

"Look at your reflection, Ned!"
call the birds together.

And then he sees ...

an orange beak,

a neck so sleek

and beautiful WHITE feathers.

Ned's as happy as can be,
  with somewhere to belong.
Says Ned, "I'm free just to be me:
  no duck – I'm Ned the SWAN!"

What happens next?

Some of the pictures from the story have been mixed up! Can you retell the story and point to each picture in the correct order?

Rhyming words

Read the words in the middle of each group and point to the other words that rhyme with them.

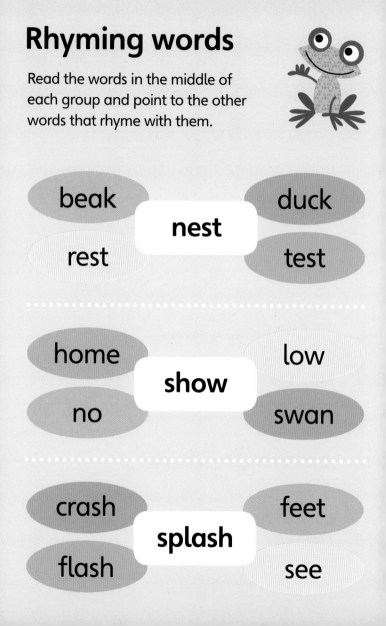

beak

nest

duck

rest

test

home

show

low

no

swan

crash

splash

feet

flash

see

been

bird

beak

sleek

weak

bed

bend

friend

mend

sock

beep

sheep

sleep

star

wake

Now choose a word and make up a rhyming chant!

The **sheep beep** when they go to **sleep!**

Key words

These sentences use common words to describe the story. Read the sentences and then make up new sentences for the other words in the border.

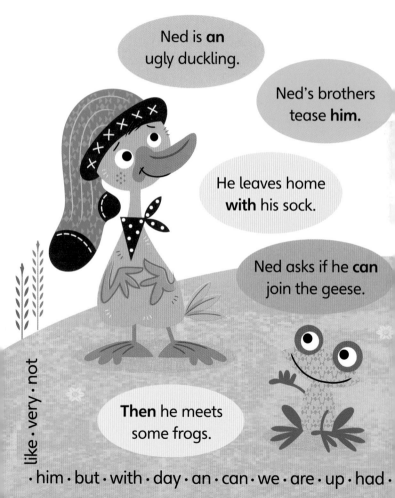

Ned is **an** ugly duckling.

Ned's brothers tease **him.**

He leaves home **with** his sock.

Ned asks if he **can** join the geese.

Then he meets some frogs.

like · very · not

· him · but · with · day · an · can · we · are · up · had ·

Picture dictionary

Look carefully at the pictures and the words.
Now cover the words, one at a time.
Can you remember how to write them?

beak

duckling

egg

feather

magpie

neck

pond

sign

swan